Welcome to The Giggle Club

The Giggle Club is a series of picture books made to put a giggle into early reading. There are funny stories about a contrary mouse, a dancing fox, a turtle with a trumpet, a pig with a ball, a hungry monster, a laughing lobster, an elephant who sneezes away the jungle, and lots more! Each of these characters is a member of **The Giggle Club**, but anyone can join: just pick up a **Giggle Club** book, read it, and get giggling!

Turn to the checklist on the inside back cover and check off the Giggle Club books you have read.

TEE HEE!

HA HA!

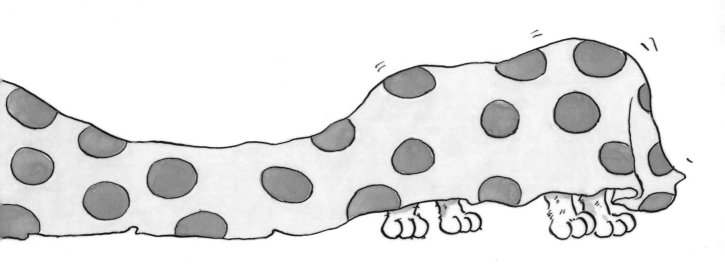

With thanks to Kate Weller! **J. H.**

For Rosina **P. C.**

Text copyright © 1998 by Judy Hindley
Illustrations copyright © 1998 by Patricia Casey

All rights reserved.

First U.S. paperback edition 1998

Library of Congress Cataloging-in-Publication Data

Hindley, Judy.
The best thing about a puppy / Judy Hindley ; illustrated by Patricia Casey.
— 1st U.S. ed.
p.   cm.
Summary: A young boy describes all the things he likes and
does not like about his feisty new puppy.
ISBN 0-7636-0596-4 (hardcover). — ISBN 0-7636-0597-2 (paperback)
[1 Dogs — Fiction.] I. Casey, Patricia, ill. II. Title.
PZ7.H5696Bg   1998
[E] — dc21   97-40292

10 9 8 7 6 5 4 3 2

Printed in Hong Kong

This book was typeset in AT Arta.
The pictures were done in watercolor and ink.

Candlewick Press
2067 Massachusetts Avenue
Cambridge, Massachusetts 02140

THE BEST THING ABOUT A PUPPY

Judy Hindley

illustrated by Patricia Casey

CANDLEWICK PRESS
CAMBRIDGE, MASSACHUSETTS

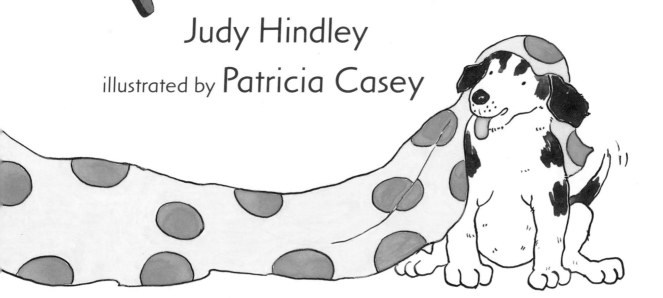

The good
thing about a
puppy is,
he's warm
and
wriggly.

The bad thing is,
he won't
keep still.

The good thing is,
the way he
rolls and
bounces.

The bad thing is,
he goes and jumps
in puddles — and then
he bounces back
and shakes himself and
wants to cuddle.

The good thing is,

you get to walk him every day.

The bad thing is,

he wants to go his own way.

The good thing is,
he loves to
chase a ball.

The bad thing is, he hates to
give it back.

The good thing is,
he likes to race
with you.

The bad thing is,

he trips you!

The good thing is,
he knows just when
to comfort you.

The bad thing is,
he licks your hands
and then your
face and neck
and ears —

shoo,
puppy!
Shoo!

Sometimes when you call, he will not come.

And then you have to call and call and look for him.

But when you find
your puppy,

you're so glad!

The best thing is,
a puppy is a friend.

Woof! Woof!
Get off me, pup!

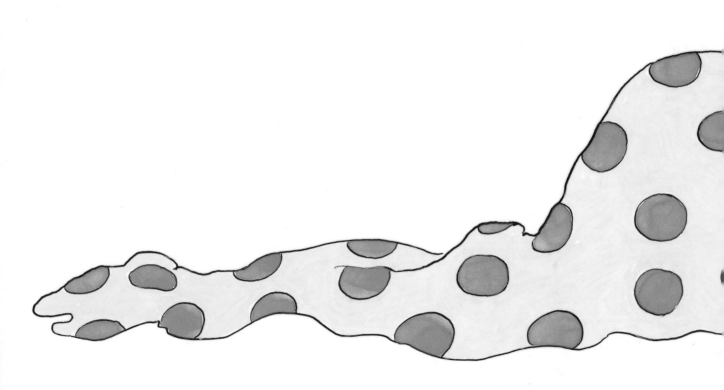